THE WILD SWANS
by Hans Christian Andersen
Translated from the original Danish text by Marlee Alex
Illustrated by Juan Alonzo Diaz Toledo
First U.S. Edition 1985 by Barron's Educational Series, Inc.
Text: ©Copyright 1984 Scandinavia Publishing House, Noerregade 32.DK-1165 K.
Artwork: ©Copyright 1984 J.R. Alonzo Diaz Toledo and Scandinavia Publishing House

All inquiries should be addressed to:
Barron's Educational Series, Inc.
113 Crossways Park Drive
Woodbury, New York 11797

Library of Congress Catalog Card No. 85-18676
International Standard Book No. 0-8120-5711-2
Printed In Italy
567 987654321

The Wild Swans

Hans Christian Andersen

Illustrated by Juan Alonso Diaz-Toledo
Translated from the original text
by Marlee Alex

BARRON'S

Woodbury, New York

Far, far away, where the swallows fly in the winter, lived a King who had eleven sons and one daughter, Elisa. When the eleven Princes went to school they wore stars on their chests and carried swords at their sides. They wrote on golden tablets with diamond pencils and could recite their lessons by heart. Their sister Elisa sat on a little chair made of mirror-glass and looked at a picture book which had cost half the kingdom.

The children were very fortunate, but it wouldn't always remain like that.

Their father married a wicked Queen who was not at all good to the poor children. Things were different from the very first day. The palace had been decorated, so the children played house in the courtyard, but instead of getting all the cakes and roasted apples they wished, she gave them only sand in a teacup and told them just to pretend it was something better.

A week later she sent Elisa to live with some peasants in the country. And it wasn't long before the Queen had influenced the King so that he didn't care at all for the eleven Princes any longer.

8

"Fly out into the world and take care of yourselves!" screamed the wicked Queen to the brothers. "Fly like great birds without voices!". But she was not able to put as terrible a curse on them as she wished. With a strange cry they flew out of the palace windows and over the forest.

While it was still early morning they flew over the cottage where their sister Elisa was sleeping. Swerving over the rooftop they craned their long necks and flapped their wings, but no one heard or saw them. So away they flew, into the clouds and the wide world.

In the peasant cottage poor little Elisa played with a leaf, for she hadn't any other toys. She made a hole in the leaf and looked through it up at the sun. It reminded her of the bright eyes of her brothers. And each time the warm sunbeams shone on her cheeks she thought of all their kisses.

One day passed just like the other. The wind blew through the big rose hedge outside and whispered to the roses, "Who can be more beautiful than you?" But the roses shook their heads and said, "Elisa is!" On Sundays the peasant woman sat in the doorway and read her psalmbook. The wind rippled the pages and said to the book, "Who can be more devout than you?" "Elisa is!" said the psalmbook. And it was perfectly true.

When she was fifteen years old Elisa was brought home to the palace. The Queen was angry and spiteful when she saw how beautiful Elisa had grown. She would have changed her to a wild swan like her brothers, but she dared not do it because the King wished to see his daughter.

Early one morning the Queen went into the marble bathroom that was decorated with soft cushions and lush carpets. She took three toads with her, kissed them, and said to the first, "Sit on Elisa's head when she comes to bathe, so that she becomes lazy like you!" To the second she commanded, "Sit on her forehead, so that she becomes ugly and her father will not recognize her." To the third she whispered, "Rest upon her heart, so that she may be tormented by an evil mind."

Then she put the toads into the clear water. It turned green immediately. She called Elisa and told her to undress and go down into the water. When Elisa entered the water the first toad sat in her hair, the second on her forehead, and the third on her breast. But it seemed as if Elisa took no notice. As soon as she got out again, three red poppies floated on the water. If the toads had not been made

poisonous by the kiss of the witch, they would have become red roses.

But they did at least become flowers just by resting upon Elisa's head and heart. She was so pure and innocent that the magic had no power over her.

When the wicked Queen saw this, she rubbed Elisa's skin with walnut juice until it became dark brown. She wiped her beautiful face with a smelly lotion and let it tangle her lovely hair. It was impossible to recognize Elisa.

When her father saw her, he exclaimed, "This girl cannot be my daughter!" No one recognized her except the dog and the swallows, but they were mere animals and so couldn't say a word. Elisa sobbed. She longed for her eleven absent brothers. Sadly, she slipped out of the palace and walked over the fields and through the marshland toward the forest.

12

She hadn't the least idea where she was going. She was brokenhearted and decided to look for her brothers; she imagined they had probably been driven from the castle just as she had been.

Elisa entered the forest only a short time before nightfall. She left the pathway, lay down on the dim moss, and said her evening prayer. It was very quiet. The air was warm, and around about the place where she lay, hundreds of glowworms shone like green firelight. When she softly touched one of the branches, the glow-worms fell like shooting stars.

14

Throughout the night Elisa dreamed of her brothers. In her dreams they played again as children, wrote with diamond pencils on golden tablets, and looked at the picture book which had cost half the kingdom. But they didn't merely draw numbers and sketches as they had before. Instead, they wrote the loveliest poems about all they had done, seen, and heard. And in the picture book, everything was living. The birds sang aloud, and the people left the pages of the book and spoke to Elisa and her brothers. When she turned the pages, they jumped in again so that the pictures wouldn't get mixed up.

When Elisa awoke, the sun was so high she couldn't see it behind the dense trees. But the sunbeams played around her like sprinkled gold dust. There was a fragrance of greenery, and the birds fluttered near her shoulder. She heard water bubbling like a fountain, and, following the sound, came to a pond fed by many large springs. Thick bushes grew around it, but at one place the deer had dug an opening, and Elisa crawled through it down to the water. The water was so clear that if the bushes and branches had not been swaying with the wind, she would have thought they were painted on the bottom, for each leaf was reflected in detail.

When Elisa saw the reflection of her own face, she was frightened for it was so brown and ugly! She rubbed her eyes and forehead with water until her white skin shone through. Then she undressed and swam into the fresh water to bathe. A lovelier princess could not be found anywhere in the whole world.

Dressed again, Elisa braided her long hair and drank of the bubbling fountain, then wandered farther into the forest. She thought about her brothers and about her loving Lord, who surely would not forsake her. It was he who had made wild apple trees to satisfy the hungry, and who showed her a certain tree with branches weighted down by fruit. Here she ate lunch, then put props under the tree's branches before continuing into the darkest part of the forest.

It was so quiet she could hear the sound of her own footsteps and of each little withered leaf that crunched beneath her feet. There was not a single bird to be seen, not a beam of light penetrating the large, intertwining tree branches. The tree trunks were so close to each other that when she looked straight ahead it was as if she were shut in by a fence. She felt a loneliness she had never known before.

The night was very dark. Not a single glowworm shone in the moss. Sadly, she lay down to sleep.

The next day, Elisa met an old woman who gave her some berries from a basket. Elisa asked if she had seen eleven Princes riding through the forest.

''No,'' said the old woman, ''but yesterday I saw eleven swans wearing golden crowns swimming in the stream close to here.'' She led Elisa a bit farther to a bank over a curving stream. The trees on the shore spread their long, leafy branches over the water toward each other. And where they could not reach, they had pulled their roots out of the soil to lean farther across.

Elisa said good bye to the old woman and walked beside the stream until she came to an open beach. The great ocean lay before the young girl, but there was not a boat or ship in sight. How was she to go farther? She studied the countless small stones on the beach. The water had made them round and smooth. Glass, iron, and granite had taken on the character of the water, and had become softer than her delicate hand. ''The ocean is tireless at polishing these hard stones. I will be just as tireless! Thank you for your wisdom, rolling waves! My heart tells me that one day you will carry me to my dear brothers.''

Along with the seaweed that had been washed ashore were eleven white swan feathers. Elisa gathered them into a bouquet. There was a drop of water on each of them; whether it was dew or a teardrop no one could see. It was lonesome along the beach but Elisa didn't feel lonely for the ocean was constantly changing, more than the inland lakes did in an entire year. If a large cloud rolled over, it was as if the ocean wanted to say: I can also look dark and angry. And then the wind blew and the waves turned their white side out. But if the sky was red and the wind slept, the ocean was soft as a rose petal. But no matter how quietly it rested, there was always a gentle movement along the beach as the water softly heaved like the breast of a sleeping child.

When the sun was close to setting, Elisa saw eleven wild swans wearing golden crowns flying toward land. They glided one after the other like a long, white ribbon. Elisa climbed upon the cliff and hid behind a bush. The swans landed close to her flapping their large white wings.

As the sun sank below the water, their swan feathers fell away suddenly, and there stood eleven Princes—Elisa's brothers. She cried out in joy, for even though they had changed she knew it was them, she felt it must be them. She jumped into their arms and called them by name. They were overjoyed when they saw and recognized their little sister, who had grown up and was so lovely. They laughed together, and soon they understood how wickedly their stepmother had treated them all.

The eldest brother explained, "We fly as wild swans while the sun stays in the sky. When it disappears we become human again, so we have to be careful always to be on land at sunset. If we were flying we would fall to our deaths. We don't live here, but in a country just as beautiful as this on the other side of the ocean, a great distance from here. There are no islands on the way where we can spend the night, except for a lonely little rock sticking up in the middle of the sea. It is only large enough for us to stand side by side to rest. If the sea is rough, water sprays over us. But we thank God for it; otherwise, we could never visit our dear Fatherland.

"We use the two longest days of the year to make our flight and can stay only eleven days. Here we fly over the castle where we were born and where Father lives, and over the church tower where Mother is buried. It seems as if the bushes and trees are our family, as well as the wild horses that run over the plains. The gypsies sing the old songs we danced to as children. We are drawn to come here once a year, and now we have found you, our dear little sister. We dare to stay only two days longer before we fly away again. But how can we take you with us? We have neither ship nor boat."

"How can I deliver you from this curse?" asked Elisa.

That night they talked for hours, sleeping very little.

21

Elisa was awakened by the sound of swan wings rushing above her. The brothers flew in a circle and at last flew away. But the youngest of them stayed behind. He laid his head in Elisa's lap and she stroked his white wings. They were together all day until the others returned. When the sun set, the swans were men again.

"Tomorrow we shall fly away and not return for a whole year, but we could never leave you behind. Do you have the courage to go with us? If the arms of one of us are strong enough to carry you through the forest, shouldn't our wings be strong enough together to carry you over the ocean?"

"Yes, take me with you!" exclaimed Elisa.

They spent the whole night braiding a large strong net of soft reeds and willow bark. Elisa fell asleep upon it, and when the sun rose and the brothers were changed to wild swans, they took the net in their beaks and flew high into the clouds with their sleeping sister.

The sunbeams fell onto her face, so one of the swans flew over her head and spread his wings above her for shade.

They were far from land when Elisa woke up. She thought she was still dreaming for it seemed so strange to be carried high through the air over the ocean. Beside her lay a branch with delicious ripe berries and a bunch of sweet smelling roots that the youngest brother had gathered for her. She smiled thankfully to him, for she knew it was the one who had flown over her head and shaded her with his wings.

They were so high that the first ship they saw beneath them looked like a seagull sitting on the water. The cloud behind them resembled a huge mountain, and Elisa watched the shadows of herself and her eleven brothers fly across it like giants. It was a sight more wonderful than any she had ever seen before. But as the sun grew higher and the cloud farther behind them, the moving shadow picture disappeared.

All day long they flew as an arrow rushing through the air. Actually, they were slower than usual, since they had their little sister to carry. Evening grew close, and Elisa watched the sun sink with fear in her heart. The lonely rock in the ocean was not to be seen, and the swans were beating their wings harder and harder. Elisa felt it was her fault that they had not made better time. She prayed in desperation, but still she didn't spy the rock. Black clouds closed in around them, strong gusts of wind foretold a storm, lightning flashed against the sky again and again.

The sun was now on the edge of the sea, and Elisa's heart trembled. Suddenly, the swans dove downward, and she thought they were falling until they began to glide again. When the sun was half way beneath the horizon she spied the little rock beneath them. It looked no larger than a seal pup sticking his head up above the waves. The sun sank quickly until it was only a star, then her foot touched the ground. The last spark of the sun went out like a bit of burning paper. Arm in arm her brothers stood around her as the sea beat against the rock. The heavens were shining like fire, and the thunder rolled. Elisa and her brothers held hands and sang a psalm that comforted and encouraged them.

At dawn the air was quiet. As soon as the sun rose, the swans flew away again with Elisa. The ocean was still rough. From high in the air the white foam on the black-green waves looked like millions of floating swans.

As the sun grew higher, Elisa saw before her a mountainous land crowned by shining ice caps. In the center a mile long castle, with one intricate pillar after another, stood above a beach of waving palm trees and flowers as large as millwheels. She asked if that were the country for which they were heading, but the swans shook their heads. What she saw was the Morning Princess's constantly changing castle of clouds. The swans did not dare to bring a human there.

As Elisa stared at it, the mountains crumbled and the castle collapsed, and in their place stood twelve proud churches, exactly alike, with high towers and pointed windows. She thought she heard an organ chiming, but it was only the ocean. When they approached, the churches took on the appearance of a fleet of ships sailing below, but it was really the ocean fog rolling over the water. Before her eyes everything was eternally changing.

Then Elisa saw the real land. They came upon a lovely blue mountain covered by cedar forests, villages, and castles. Long before the sun went down she sat on the mountainside in front of a large cave overgrown with green vines. It looked like an embroidered tapestry.

"Now we shall see what you will dream of tonight!" said the youngest brother, as he showed her to her sleeping chamber.

"If only I might dream of how I could rescue you!" she answered. The thought of it captivated her mind and heart. She prayed earnestly to God for help, and kept on praying as she fell asleep.

It seemed to her that she flew through the air to the castle of the Morning Princess, where a beautiful glittering fairy met her. The fairy resembled the old woman who had given her berries in the forest and told her about the eleven swans wearing golden crowns.

"Your brothers can be rescued!" she promised. "But do you have courage and endurance? The ocean is softer than your hands and yet can transform the hardest stones. But it does not feel the pain your fingers will feel. It has no heart and does not suffer the fear and anxiety which you must endure.

"Do you see these nettles I hold in my hand? There are many such nettles growing around the cave where you are sleeping. Only these and the ones growing in church-yards are usable. Although they will sting until blisters appear, you must pick the nettles and crush them with your feet into flax, then knit eleven long sleeved shirts. When you throw these shirts over the eleven wild swans, the curse will be broken. But remember—from the moment you begin the task until it is finished, though years may pass, you may not speak. The first word you say will drive a knife into your brothers' hearts. The lives of your brothers depend upon your tongue.

The fairy touched Elisa's hand with nettles that stung like little flames, and Elisa woke up. It was daylight, and close beside her lay a nettle like the one she had seen in the dream. She fell on her knees, gave thanks to the Lord, and went outside to begin her work.

Her delicate hands grabbed the stinging nettles. They burned like fire and blistered her hands and arms. She suffered the pain gladly, however, thinking only of salvation for her dear brothers. She crushed each nettle with her bare feet and spun green twine from them.

When the sun went down, her brothers returned to the cave and were frightened at finding Elisa so silent. They thought it must be due to a new curse of their evil stepmother. But when they saw her hands, they understood that what she was doing was for their sake. The youngest brother cried, and where his tears fell, the pain and the blisters disappeared.

All night long Elisa worked, for she would never have peace of heart before she had set her brothers free. All the next day, while the swans were away, she sat alone, but time had never flown so quickly. She finished one shirt and began on the next.

Suddenly, the horn of a group of hunters rang through the mountains. Elisa grew afraid as the sound of barking dogs came closer. She hurried into the cave, tying the nettles she had gathered into a bundle.

At that moment a large dog jumped out of the thicket, followed by another, and another. They barked loudly, running back and forth. Before long the hunters stood before the opening of the cave; the most handsome among them was the King. He stepped over to Elisa. Never had he seen a more beautiful girl.

"What are you doing here, you lovely child?" he asked. Elisa shook her head. She dared not speak, for the lives of her brothers depended on it. She hid her hands under her apron so the King would not see how she suffered.

"Follow me!" he commanded. "You must not stay here. If you are as sweet as you are beautiful, I will have you dressed in silk and velvet, and have a golden crown set on your head. You shall live in my regal palace."

He lifted Elisa up on his horse as she cried and wrung her hands, but the King explained: "I only want to make you happy. One day you will thank me for it!" And he rode away between the mountains holding her in front of him on the horse. The other hunters followed behind them.

As the sun set, a majestic city with its churches and towers came into sight. The King led Elisa into the palace where a large water fountain splashed in the lofty marble room. Both the walls and ceiling were covered with paintings. But Elisa did not see them, for she was crying in sorrow. Passively she allowed the woman to dress her in royal robes, braid pearls into her hair, and pull dainty gloves over her blistered fingers.

When she finally appeared in all her majesty, she was so ravishingly beautiful that the court bowed deeply before her and the King proposed to make her his bride. But the Archbishop shook his head and whispered that the beautiful girl from the woods was probably a witch who had blinded their eyes and bewitched the heart of the King.

34

The King didn't listen to him. He commanded that the music chime, that there be feasting and dancing for Elisa. He led Elisa through the fragrant gardens and great rooms of the palace. However, not a smile crossed Elisa's lips, nor shone from her eyes. There was only sorrow painted upon her face. Then the King showed her to a small chamber decorated with green carpets and wallpaper. It resembled the cave where he had found her. On the floor lay the bundle of twine she had spun from the nettles, and from the ceiling hung the finished shirt. The hunters had taken it with them as a curiosity.

"Here you can dream yourself back to your former home!" said the King. "Here is the task that kept you busy. In the splendor of the palace it may amuse you to think back on your past."

When Elisa saw that which was so dear to her heart, a smile played about her lips and the blood returned to her cheeks. She thought again of the salvation of her brothers and kissed the hand of the King as he drew her to his heart. All the churchbells rang out proclaiming the wedding celebration. The lovely, silent girl from the woods was to become the Queen.

The Archbishop whispered evil words into the ear of the King, but they did not penetrate his heart. The wedding was to take place and the Archbishop himself was to set the crown on her head. He pressed the crown harshly upon her forehead until it hurt. But her sorrow over her brothers hurt far more.

Elisa did not speak, but her eyes glowed with deep love for the good and handsome King who did all he could to make her happy. She became more and more fond of him. If only she dared to confide in him and tell him why she suffered.

But silent she must remain, silently she must fulfill her task. At night she quietly left his side, went into her little chamber, and knitted one shirt after the other. When she began the seventh, she ran out of twine.

The nettles she needed grew in the churchyard, but how could she dare go out to gather them?

"Oh what is the pain in my fingers compared to that in my heart?" she thought. "I must take the risk! The Lord will not fail me!"

With fear in her heart as if it were an evil deed she was planning, she slipped out into the moonlit night, through the long winding alleys, out onto the lonesome streets and toward the churchyard. When she arrived she saw a group of hideous witches sitting on one of the gravestones. They took their tattered clothes off, and with long lean fingers dug down into the earth. Elisa had to pass close by them as they fastened their eyes upon her. But she whispered a prayer, gathered the nettles, and carried them back to the palace.

Only one person had seen her: the Archbishop. Now he was confirmed in his suspicions that she was a witch who had deceived the King and his court. The following day he told the King from the confession booth what he had seen and what he feared. And when the hard words fell from his tongue, the carved statues of the saints shook their heads as if they wanted to say: "It is not so, Elisa is innocent." But the Archbishop explained it as if they meant to bear witness against her, shaking their heads at her shame.

Two heavy tears rolled down the King's cheeks. He went home with misgiving in his heart and only pretended to sleep that night. He noticed that Elisa got up out of bed and disappeared into her green chamber. She repeated this each of the following nights, and each time he secretly followed her.

Day by day the King's expression became darker. Elisa saw it, but didn't understand why. It worried her, and she worried as well for her brothers. Her salty tears fell on the royal purple velvet and glittered like diamonds. Everyone who saw this exquisite sight envied the Queen.

Soon Elisa would be finished with her task. Only one shirt remained to be made. But she had no more twine and not a single nettle. Once again for the last time she would have go to the courtyard and pick more of them. She remembered fearfully the lonely walk and the frightful witches, but her will was set, as was her confidence in the Lord.

40

As Elisa left the palace, the King and the Archbishop followed after and watched her disappear through the gate into the churchyard. When they drew closer they saw the witches as Elisa had seen them. The King turned his face away, for he imagined that his beloved, whose head had rested upon his chest that very evening, was going to join their company.

"The people must judge her!" he exclaimed. And the people declared, "She shall be burned at the stake!"

From the splendid palace she was led into a dark, damp cell where the wind whistled through the barred windows. Instead of velvet and silk, she was given the bunch of nettles she had gathered for a pillow, and the stiff, burning shirts she had knitted for a blanket. But nothing more precious could have been given to her. She took up her task again as she prayed to God. Outside, the boys in the street sang mocking songs about her. Not a soul comforted her with a single kind word.

At the close of the day a swan wing appeared at the barred window. It was the youngest of the brothers who had found his sister. She jumped in joy because she knew that, although the coming night was to be her last, her brothers would be close by, as her task was nearly finished.

The Archbishop came to be with Elisa the last hour of her life just as he had promised the King. But Elisa shook her head at him and begged in sign language to be left alone. Tonight she must finish work or everything would be in vain—the pain, the tears, the sleepless nights. The Archbishop left with evil words about her, but the poor little Elisa knew she was innocent and remained at her task. Little mice ran over the floor and helped her by dragging the nettles to her feet. The thrush perched at the window-bars, singing bravely throughout the night, to keep her courage up.

At dawn, less that an hour before the sunrise, Elisa's brothers stood at the gates of the palace and demanded to be led before the King. They were refused permission on the grounds that the King could not be disturbed. They begged and they threatened until the King himself came out. But at that moment the sun rose and

Elisa's brothers were no longer there. The King saw only eleven wild swans flying low over the palace.

Townspeople streamed through the city gates, intending to see the burning of the witch. A scraggly old horse pulled the cart upon which she sat. She was dressed in rough sackcloth and her lovely long hair hung loose around her beautiful face. Her cheeks were deathly pale, but her lips moved gently as her fingers continued to knit the green twine. Even on the way to her death she refused to give up her task. Ten shirts lay at her feet as she worked on the eleventh. The crowd jeered.

"Look at the witch! See how she mumbles! She carries no psalmbook in her hand but only her gruesome witchcraft! Tear it from her hands and into a thousand pieces!"

The crowd pressed close to the cart and would have grabbed the nettle shirt, but the eleven white swans appeared and flew at them. The swans sat around Elisa on the cart and flapped their powerful wings, forcing the mob to the side.

"It is a sign from Heaven. She must be innocent," whispered many. but they dared not say it aloud.

As the executioner grabbed Elisa by the hand, she quickly threw the eleven shirts over the swans. Suddenly in their places stood eleven Princes. The youngest, however, had a swan wing instead of an arm, for Elisa had not had time to finish the last sleeve of his shirt.

"Now I will speak!" Elisa cried out.
"I am innocent!"

The people, who had watched what happened, kneeled before her as before a saint. But Elisa sank lifeless into the arms of her brothers. The fear, worry, and pain had taken its toll on her.

"Yes, she is innocent!" shouted the oldest brother. He told everything that had happened, and while he spoke a fragrance floated through the air. It was like the perfume of a million roses, for every piece of kindling at the stake had taken root and sent forth branches, until it became a sweet smelling hedge covered with red roses. At the top a single white flower bloomed, shining and radiant as a star. The King picked it and laid in on Elisa's breast. She woke up with peace and happiness in her heart.

All the church bells started ringing by themselves, and birds flew around in large flocks escorting the procession back to the castle. It was more festive that any king had ever seen.

43